Surf's Up, Pikachu!

POKÉMON
junior

(#1)

Surf's Up, Pikachu!

#1 POKÉMON junior™

Adapted by Bill Michaels

SCHOLASTIC INC.
New York Toronto London Auckland Sydney
Mexico City New Delhi Hong Kong

No part of this publication may be reproduced in whole or in part, or stored in a retrieval system, or transmitted in any form or by any means, electronic, mechanical, photocopying, recording, or otherwise, without written permission of the publisher. For information regarding permission, write to Scholastic Inc., Attention: Permissions Department, 555 Broadway, New York, NY 10012.

ISBN 0-439-15405-7

12 11 10 9 8 7 6 5   0 1 2 3 4 5 6/0

Printed in the U.S.A.

First Scholastic printing, May 2000

Surf's Up, Pikachu!

Pokémon junior

#1

**There are more books
about Pokémon for
younger readers.**

COLLECT THEM ALL!

#1 Surf's Up, Pikachu!

#2 Meowth, the Big Mouth

COMING SOON!

#3 Save Our Squirtle!

CHAPTER ONE

"Watch Out, Ash!"

Pikachu was running fast. But Ash was running faster. Ash was Pikachu's trainer. They were at the beach on Seafoam Island. They were training to become Pokémon masters.

But this running was hard! Pikachu wanted to slow down and

play in the water. Ash did not

want to.

He wanted to

be the best

Pokémon trainer

in the world.

Ash was traveling with his

friends Misty and Brock. Pikachu

and Togepi were with them.

Togepi was a little Pokémon.

It went wherever Misty went.

Pikachu was Ash's Pokémon.

It went wherever Ash went.

Ash loved all his Pokémon.

But Pikachu was his first one.

It was special to him. And Pikachu loved Ash, too.

Just then, Pikachu saw a puddle of oil on the crowded road. It was right in front of Ash. *Oh, no!* thought Pikachu. *Ash is going to slip in that puddle!*

"*Pika! Pika pi!*" cried Pikachu. *Watch out, Ash!*

But it was too late. Ash slipped on the puddle. He stumbled into the street. All the cars behind him stopped. They honked their horns.

Pikachu knew that Ash felt bad.

He did not mean to stop traffic.

"Pika pika," Pikachu said.

It is okay. I am glad you are not hurt.

Pikachu helped Ash stand up. Officer Jenny came to help him. All the cars drove away.

Ash asked Officer Jenny why there were so many cars with surfboards. "Lots of surfers are here," she said. "They want to surf a big wave. It is called Humungadunga. It comes only once every twenty years."

"Wow!" said Ash.

"Pika pika pi!" said Pikachu.
Pikachu could not imagine a wave
so big it had its own name!

"Why do they want to surf that
big wave?" asked Misty.

Pikachu could not wait to
hear the story. It jumped up on
Ash's shoulder to hear Officer
Jenny talk.

CHAPTER TWO

The Story of Jan

"They want to be like the
greatest surfer of all time," Officer
Jenny began. "His name was Jan.
Forty years ago, he surfed
Humungadunga. He put his flag
on that big rock."

Officer Jenny pointed out
to sea.

Pikachu looked out at the ocean. There was a big rock out there. It was very tall and very far away. On top of the rock was a flag. The flag had a "J" on it, for Jan. How could anyone ever reach that high?

"No one has done that since Jan did it," said Officer Jenny.

Ash looked out at the rock and the flag. Pikachu could tell its trainer wanted to surf out to the rock. He wanted to put a flag on it, just like Jan!

"Ash, what about your training?" Misty said.

"I *am* training, Misty. I am training to be the world's best surfer, like Jan!" said Ash.

Ash was carrying his surfboard. He ran into the water. Misty and Brock went, too. Pikachu played on the shore with Togepi.

Togepi splashed Pikachu.

"Pika pi!" said Pikachu. *Playing in the sand is fun!*

"Brrrrrrrr-brrrrrrrr," said Togepi. It was pointing to the sky.

Pikachu looked up. There was another Pikachu on top of a high cliff. The other Pikachu looked just like Ash's Pikachu. But Ash's Pikachu could tell there was something very special about it. The other Pikachu was looking out to sea. Its tail was trembling. Its ears were moving. The Pikachu seemed to know something about the ocean.

Pikachu wondered if it could go talk to the other Pikachu.

The cliff was high up, but . . .

Just then, Pikachu heard Ash out in the waves. He kept falling off his surfboard.

"Brrrrrrrr!" said Togepi, laughing. *Look at Ash!*

But it was not funny. Ash had hurt his foot on the surfboard. Pikachu could tell that Ash was in trouble. If Ash did not get help soon, he would drown!

CHAPTER THREE

Puka to the Rescue

Pikachu knew Ash was in danger. But Pikachu did not know how to save its trainer. It could not swim to him in time.

Then Pikachu heard the other Pikachu. It was shouting, *"Pika!"* *Victor — come quick! Someone is hurt!*

A man ran out of the cabin on
the cliff. He had long gray hair.
He was wearing swimming trunks.
He carried a red surfboard.
"Right, Puka," he said to the other
Pikachu. "Looks like someone
could use our help."

Victor and Puka shot into the
water on the red surfboard.

"Hang on! We will save you!"
shouted Victor.

Pikachu could hardly look.
Oh, please let Ash be okay,
thought Pikachu.

Victor and Puka surfed out

to Ash. Pikachu and Togepi watched. *"Pika,"* whispered Pikachu. *I am so worried.*

On the surfboard, Victor told Puka what to do. "Shoot the curl, Puka!" cried Victor. "Puka, pipeline!"

Puka was a great surfer! It brought the surfboard right to Ash. Victor pulled Ash onboard. At last he was safe!

Ash put his head down on the surfboard. He looked up

for a moment at Puka. He thought he was seeing his Pikachu!

"Pika . . . chu?" Ash gasped. Then he fainted.

"Pika pika pi!" cried Puka. *Another great rescue!*

CHAPTER FOUR

"Steal One, Get One Free"

Victor and Puka brought Ash to Victor's cabin. It took a long time for Ash to wake up.

Pikachu waited for him.

Finally, Ash opened his eyes.

"Pika pika chu chu," said Pikachu. *I thought I would never see you again.*

"Oh, Pikachu," said Ash. He gave Pikachu a hug. They were quiet for a moment.

Misty and Brock told Ash all about the daring rescue. "Victor is the reason you are still here. He saved your life," said Brock.

"No need to thank me," said Victor. "Thank my Pikachu, Puka."

Pikachu went to find Puka. The other Pikachu was out on the cliff. It was looking out at the sea.

"Pika pika," said Pikachu. *Thank you for saving Ash.*

He is my best friend.

"*Pika chu chu,*" said Puka.

It was all because of Victor. He is a great surfer.

Pikachu and Puka were happy talking. So they did not notice that Ash's enemies, Team Rocket, were watching them. Team Rocket worked for a man who collected rare Pokémon. They knew Pikachu was a special Pokémon. So they were always trying to take it away from Ash.

Jessie, James, and their Pokémon Meowth were hiding in a submarine. The submarine was specially built to look like a Gyarados!

"Am I seeing double?" asked Jessie. She was looking through a periscope. "Or are there two Pikachu on that cliff?"

"Steal one, get one free!" said James.

"*Meowth!* The boss will love us," added Meowth.

"Maybe he will give *double* our

pay. Or a *two*-week vacation," said James.

"Full steam ahead for Pikachu times two!" cried Jessie.

"Aye-aye, sir!" said Meowth.

CHAPTER FIVE

A Pokémon From the Sea

Inside the cabin, Victor was telling Ash, Misty, and Brock about Puka.

"Hush now, Togepi," whispered Misty to her little Pokémon. "Time for your nap." She wanted to hear Victor's story.

"I did not capture Puka the way

you capture a regular Pokémon," said Victor. "Puka came to me from the sea. It was like I called out, and Puka heard me. I was sitting by the shore, watching the waves. Suddenly there was Puka. It was floating toward me on a little raft. I looked into its eyes. I knew we were meant to be together."

"Wow," said Ash.

"I cannot explain how or why it happened, but from that day on,

Puka and I have never been apart."

"How mysterious!" said Misty.

"Yes," replied Victor. "Puka is very mysterious."

"What do you mean?" asked Ash.

"Puka can feel the waves in its body," said Victor. "It can always tell when a big wave is coming. That is why Puka and I have surfed together for almost twenty years."

Twenty years! thought

Ash. *That is forever!*

Misty was looking at the pictures in Victor's cabin. There were pictures of Victor from a long time ago.

"And who is that?" asked Brock, pointing to a picture of a young man with a surfboard.

"That is Jan," said Victor. "A surfer named Jan."

"Huh?" said Ash.

"I started surfing because of Jan," said Victor. "I wanted to be just like him. He was the best."

Victor told Ash and his friends

all about Jan. "Jan helped me. I was just learning to surf. I fell off my board a lot. But Jan never made fun of me," Victor said.

"Jan surfed Humungadunga. He was the only one to do that! He planted his flag in the great rock. And he told me that I would do the same thing one day."

Victor hung his head.

"What is the matter?" asked Misty.

"Twenty years ago, I tried to surf Humungadunga. But I was not good enough. That has been

the greatest sadness of my life."

Victor was quiet for a moment.

"But then Puka came to me. Maybe that is why we found each other. So that we can surf Humungadunga together."

"I know you can!" said Ash.

Just then, they heard screams coming from the cliff. Something bad was happening to the two Pikachu!

CHAPTER SIX

Dragon Rage

"Prepare for trouble."

"Make it double."

Oh, no! thought Ash. *It is Team Rocket!*

Jessie and James had captured the Pikachu. Two huge mechanical arms held the Pokémon over the edge of the cliff!

"*Pikaaa!*" cried Pikachu. *Help!*
Help us!

Ash almost jumped off the cliff.
He had to save Pikachu! But
Brock and Misty stopped him just
in time.

Jessie and
James and
Meowth used
the mechanical
arms to take the
two Pikachu into
their Gyarados submarine.
There was nothing Ash
could do!

Inside the submarine, Pikachu tried to get free. *"Pika pika pi!"* it shouted. *Get off me!* But Team Rocket stuffed the two Pikachu into a glass cage.

"Pik-a-chu!" cried Pikachu. *We can use our lightning power to escape!*

The two Pikachu used all their energy. They sent out lightning shock after lightning shock. But it was no use. They could not break out.

They were trapped.

"Do not waste your energy," said Meowth.

"That little capture capsule is one hundred percent shockproof!" said Jessie.

But then James noticed something very scary. Dozens of fierce Gyarados Pokémon were circling the submarine. Their red eyes glowed in the dark sea.

"Gyarados!" cried Jessie.

"What are they doing here?" said Meowth.

"Well, I *have* heard that

Gyarados travel to shallow waters once a year. That is where they lay their eggs," said James.

The Gyarados plowed into the sub.

"They are ramming us!" shouted Meowth.

"During egg-laying season, Gyarados do not like company," James added.

"We have to get out of here!" cried Jessie.

"Aye-aye, sir!" said James and Meowth.

But the Gyarados were angry.

They used their massive Dragon Rage Attack to teach the invaders a lesson.

Team Rocket tried to escape. But the Gyarados zapped the sub. It flew out of the sea and cracked in half! Team Rocket screamed and disappeared far, far into the distance.

CHAPTER SEVEN

Humungadunga

But Pikachu and Puka were
still in danger! The blast from the
Gyarados shattered their cage.
The two Pikachu flew through the
air. Now they were going to crash
into the raging water!

"Pika!" cried Pikachu. *Ash!*
Help!

Ash was nearby in Victor's boat with Brock and Misty. They were coming to rescue their Pikachu!

Ash threw a Poké Ball into the air. Out came Bulbasaur, a Grass Pokémon! "Bulbasaur, Vine Whip, now!"

"Bulbasaur!" it cried.

Bulbasaur wrapped its powerful vine around Pikachu. It was just in time to save Pikachu from the stormy waters.

But Puka was still not safe. The ocean was wild. Even Puka was in danger of drowning! Pikachu saw Victor throw Puka his surfboard. Then he tore off his shirt and jumped into the water to save Puka.

Oh, no! thought Pikachu. *The water is too rough! Can Victor get to Puka in time?*

But Victor fought the waves. He was a good

swimmer. He grabbed his Pikachu. The two landed safely on Victor's surfboard.

Just then, there was a great roar. Pikachu had never heard anything like it before. Puka's tail trembled. The Pikachu looked at Victor. They both nodded.

"Humungadunga! Here it comes!" screamed Victor.

Puka and Victor knew it was time.

CHAPTER EIGHT

Victory!

Ash, Pikachu, and the others watched from the beach. They held their breath. Victor was trying to surf the big wave!

"Go, dudes!" yelled Brock.

You can do it! thought Pikachu.

Pikachu saw Victor and Puka

catch the wave. Up, up, up, higher and higher they rose. Then they were flying over the top of the rock. Puka steered the surfboard.

Victor used all his strength to plant his flag right next to Jan's.

"Augh!" he cried as the flagpole sank into the hard stone.

"Pikaaaaa!" shouted Puka.

Victory! A new legend was born!

"*Pika pi!*" cried Pikachu with joy. *You made it!*

"*Pi pi pika!*" came the faint reply from Puka. *We did it!*

———

When Victor and Puka reached the shore, Pikachu, Ash, and their friends were waiting. "Victor, that was awesome!" said Ash.

"*Pika pika chu chu,*" Pikachu

told Puka. *You are truly a great surfer. I am so proud of you.*

"*Pika pi!*" said Puka. *Victor and I did it together.*

"*Chu chu,*" Pikachu replied. *You make a great team!*

At that moment, Victor spotted a little boy and girl on the beach. They were looking at Victor's red surfboard.

"Here you go, kids," said Victor. "It is time for me to move on now." He handed the board to the children. He and Puka had conquered Humungadunga. Now

they were ready for their next adventure!

"Victor's flag sure looks great on top of that rock," said Ash.

The flag flapped proudly in the breeze, right next to Jan's. It was marked with a big "V" — for Victor, and for Victory!

"Yes," said Brock. "But it is more than a flag. It is proof that it is never too late for some dreams to come true."

"Right," said Ash. "Victor and Puka certainly followed their dream." He picked up Pikachu

and gave it a hug. "Now — time for some fun." Ash grabbed his surfboard and ran into the water.

"Surf's up, Pikachu! Come on in!"

And as Misty, Togepi, and Brock watched from the shore, Ash and Pikachu rode the sparkling waves till the sun finally set on Seafoam Island.

Pikachu to the rescue!

Pokémon junior

Chapter Book #3:
Save Our Squirtle!

It's no secret that the evil Team Rocket is out to get Pikachu. But when they kidnap Squirtle to get to the little lightning mouse, they've gone too far! Can Pikachu and pals save their friend in time? Or will the tiny turtle become Team Rocket's newest member?

Coming soon to a bookstore near you!

Visit us at www.scholastic.com

SCHOLASTIC